VIKING

Published by the Penguin Group
Penguin Books Ltd, 27 Wrights Lane, London W8 5TZ, England
Penguin Putnam Inc., 375 Hudson Street, New York, New York 10014, USA
Penguin Books Australia Ltd, Ringwood, Victoria, Australia
Penguin Books Canada Ltd, 10 Alcorn Avenue, Toronto, Ontario, Canada M4V 3B2
Penguin Books (NZ) Ltd, Private Bag 102902, NSMC, Auckland, New Zealand

On the World Wide Web at: www.penguin.com

Penguin Books Ltd, Registered Offices: Harmondsworth, Middlesex, England

First published 2000
1 3 5 7 9 10 8 6 4 2

Printed in Singapore by Imago Publishing

British Library Cataloguing in Publication Data
A CIP catalogue record for this book is available from the British Library

ISBN 0–670–88638–6

1. Emperor penguins - Fiction. 2. Penguins - Fiction. 3. Antarctica - Fiction.

THERESA RADCLIFFE

# Nanu, Penguin Chick

*Illustrated by*
JOHN BUTLER

VIKING

All winter, fierce winds and terrible blizzards had raged across Antarctica, battering the emperor's nesting place. Through the long, dark days, Yellowneck huddled with the other penguin fathers, guarding the precious egg that Whitefeather had left in his care. At last, the egg hatched and little Nanu peeped out on to the white frozen world. From far across the ice, Yellowneck heard Whitefeather calling. She was returning with food for their young chick.

Whitefeather gently took the little chick from him. Yellowneck was weak now with hunger. He needed to return to the sea to find food. Whitefeather fed and cared for Nanu and she grew quickly. When she became too big for Whitefeather's pouch, she rode around on her mother's feet. And all this time, Whitefeather sang to her chick, so that Nanu would learn to recognize her voice. Nanu returned her calls, lifting her little neck, and whistling her replies.

As the weeks passed, Nanu began to leave her mother's side and explore the icy world around her. But this was a dangerous time for the penguin chicks, for the winter storms were not over yet. One day a harsh blizzard blew up. For a time, little Nanu was lost. She could not find her way in the blinding snow. She wandered alone through the freezing wind, calling desperately for Whitefeather.

At first, Whitefeather could not hear her chick's cries above the raging wind. She searched everywhere for her, then at last, Nanu's faint cry drifted towards her. She called back to her chick and they ran to each other. Nanu nestled safely against her mother for the rest of the storm.

At last, the weather grew warmer and Yellowneck returned to help Whitefeather take care of Nanu. They took turns making the long journey over the ice to find food. Soon the sea ice began to break up and the open water grew nearer. Leaving Nanu alone, Whitefeather and Yellowneck set out across the ice to find food for their growing chick.

Whitefeather and Yellowneck hurried towards the sea, anxious not to be away from their chick for too long. Far above them, giant icebergs shimmered and glinted in the bright sun. On and on they marched towards the open water, where the tiny shrimp-like krill teemed, food for themselves and their hungry chick. Unknown to them, out at sea, two leopard seals lay basking on the floating ice, waiting for their next meal.

W hitefeather was
first into the water and
began to make her way through the melting
ice towards the open sea. Yellowneck hesitated
for a moment on the ice edge. Then he saw them — two
huge dark shapes suddenly lunging upward through the
broken ice, their savage jaws bared. He cried a warning and
Whitefeather turned in horror. She made it back to the shore just in time.
It was a while before they dared venture into the sea again.

Back at the nesting site, Nanu was waiting anxiously with the other penguin chicks. Where were Whitefeather and Yellowneck? Why hadn't they come back? Each time a penguin parent returned with food, she ran forward, hoping it would be them. She was growing more and more hungry and desperate.

Meanwhile, Yellowneck and Whitefeather had at last made their catch and were now hurrying back over the ice to Nanu. High above them two dark shapes soared through the sky. The skuas were arriving. They had come to seek out weak and sickly chicks.

$L$ ittle Nanu was standing apart from the other
penguin chicks. She had wandered away to try
and find food herself. Suddenly above her she saw
the beating wings, the flash of sharp ugly beaks as
the huge birds swooped . . .

Yellowneck and Whitefeather had just reached the group of young penguins. They called to Nanu. She didn't reply. She didn't come running out to meet them. They searched anxiously among the other chicks. Then, in the distance, they saw the great birds bearing down on a terrified chick. They heard a cry. It was their own chick! It was little Nanu! She was in terrible danger.

Whitefeather and Yellowneck tore across the ice. The cowardly birds veered away to find an easier victim. Little Nanu was safe again. As the sun sank and the ice shimmered golden, Yellowneck and Whitefeather looked down on their little chick. She was full of food now and nestled happily to sleep between them. They had cared for her well. Little Nanu, the emperor chick, had survived her first winter.

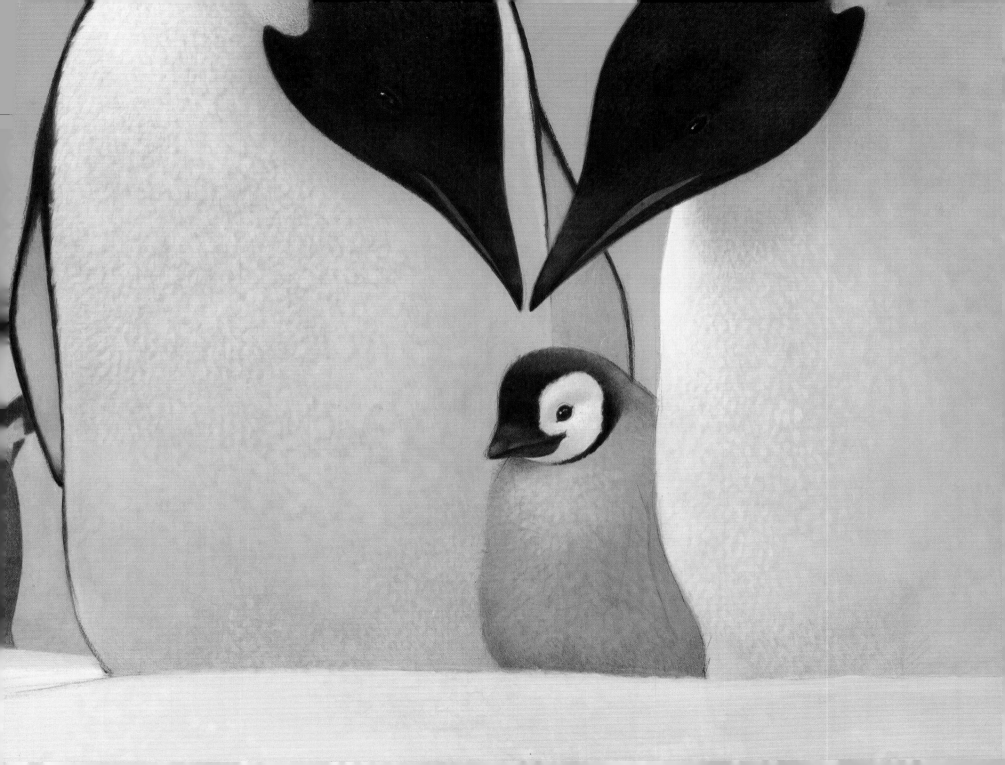